A Visit to
Fairyland

The Five Mile Press

Laura said there were fairies at the bottom of the garden. She said that in the old willow tree there was a green door and when the fairies opened it you could see right into Fairyland.

"Yes, dear," said her mother who was busy cooking. "Now, why don't you take your little brother into the garden? You can show him the fairies and the door to Fairyland."

Laura could tell that her mother thought she was just pretending and she felt rather hurt. Still, she took Daniel's hand and led him into the garden and down towards the willow tree.

"Ssh, Danny," she whispered. "If we are very quiet the fairies might open their green door and come out to talk to us."

Sure enough, after a few minutes the green door opened...and out came the fairies.

"Would you like to come through this little doorway and see Fairyland?" asked the fairies.

"Oh yes!" exclaimed Laura excitedly. Then she and Daniel crawled through the doorway and found themselves in Fairyland.

Before them was a toadstool town where pixies and other fairy folk were busy shopping and chatting, just like people. Daniel trotted off chuckling to explore the narrow twisting streets.

"Don't go too far, you might get lost," warned his sister. "Stay close so I can keep an eye on you!"

MONTY MOUSE

E. ELF

1

To Daniel the toadstool houses were just like a toy village and he wanted to play with the pixies. Laura watched him running about for a while, then she noticed further away a garden full of big flowers.

"Come along, Danny," she coaxed. "Let's go and look at those beautiful flowers."

The flowers were so large that Daniel soon forgot the toadstool houses and ran to look at them. Inside each flower a fairy baby was curled up as if in its cradle.

"This is where our babies live till they are old enough to fly," a fairy nurse told the children.

The flower nursery was bathed in warm golden light and soon the children were glad to go into some nearby woods where it was cool and shady. A fern-fringed path led them to a lily pool where fairies were bathing and playing near a crystal spring. Laura and Daniel drank spring water from leaf-cups, and paddled in the shallows. Soon they felt cool enough to explore further.

They followed the path through the woods and before long they heard sweet music: pipes, bells, and a tinkling harp. Then, in a clearing edged with flowers, they came upon a group of elfin musicians. Rabbits, mice, and frogs all had their parts to play, and several fairies were dancing to the music.

"There is a ball tonight," the fairies explained to the children, "so we are practicing our steps!"

The children wandered on and soon they came to the edge of the woods. There, between twisted tree roots, large caves had formed in a sandy bank. Inside each cave was a kitchen in which elfin cooks were preparing a marvelous feast.

"All these lovely dishes will be served at the ball tonight," the fairies told the children. "The food is cooked here, then taken to the fairy castle in butterfly carriages."

Of course the children felt hungry seeing such lovely food, so the kindly elves invited them to sit down and eat whatever they liked.

While they tried all kinds of dainty and colorful cakes and biscuits, Laura talked to the fairies and elves about life in Fairyland.

"Do you ever have to do any work?" she asked.

"Oh, yes," one silver-haired fairy replied. "My work is to go out and put frost crystals everywhere."

"Why do you do that?" Laura asked, puzzled.

"Well, when the world has been dull and gloomy, and you wake to a day where every twig and grass blade sparkles, it's suddenly a beautiful surprise, isn't it?"

"Oh yes it is," cried Laura. "Thank you, Silver Fairy, for all your lovely frosty mornings!"

"I too have my work in the world," said an elf, smiling at Laura and Daniel. "With my baskets of toadstools I fly round at first light and I plant bright red ones where I think they will look just right."

"Yes, we've seen them, haven't we, Daniel?" cried Laura excitedly. "You left some spotted ones under the pine trees just outside our garden."

"Now, what would you like to see next?" the fairies asked the children.

Laura looked at Daniel. "We ought to be going home," she said regretfully. "Our Aunt Kathy is coming to lunch at our house, and it will be ready soon."

But Daniel wasn't ready to go home, and Laura was afraid he would make a fuss, so she decided they could stay in Fairyland for just a little while longer.

"Can we see where you make all your pretty sparkling dresses?" she asked the fairies. So the fairies showed the children the little silk spinners who spend all their time making gossamer-fine shawls, cloaks, and dresses, all delicately sewn with diamond droplets.

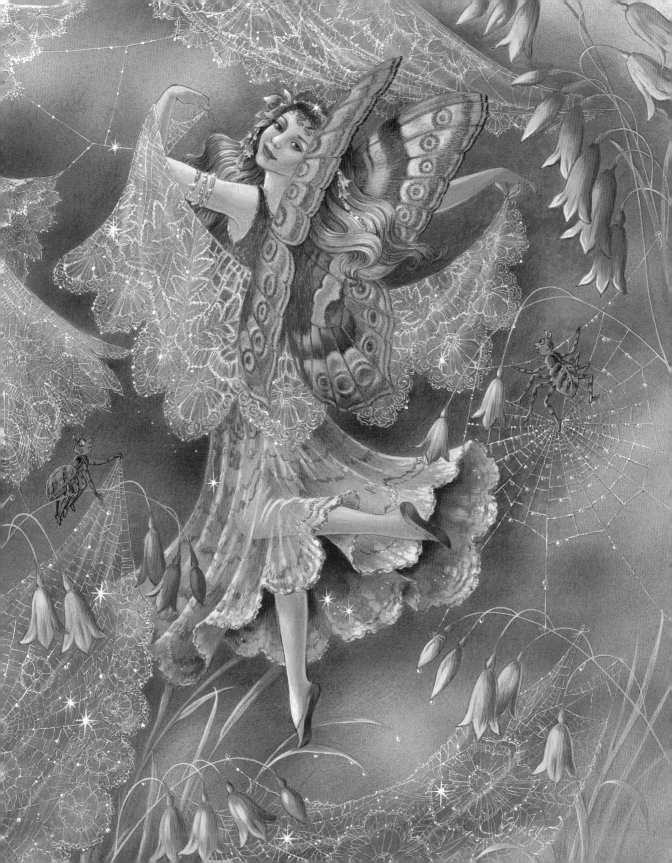

"Please show us one last thing before we go home," said Laura. "We'd love to see the fairy castle where you live and where the ball will be held tonight."

So the fairies put Laura and Daniel into a butterfly carriage which floated over the sea to a bay of islands, where a glittering fairy castle stood upon a rocky pinnacle.

While they were circling the castle, Daniel fell asleep in the butterfly carriage. It flew over the forest, the big flowers, and the toadstool town before landing at last near the old willow tree.

Laura woke up Daniel, and while he was still too sleepy to protest she helped him crawl back through the little doorway.

"Goodbye, Laura and Daniel," called the fairies. "Be good and kind, and you will see us again soon."

Then the little green door shut and seemed to fade away.

"Come along, Danny," said Laura. "Let's go and have lunch, and we'll tell Mummy all about our visit to Fairyland."

The children found their mother just laying the table for lunch. Their Aunt Kathy had arrived, and she hugged the children and gave each of them a drawing book and a packet of coloring pencils.

"Danny's very good at drawing," Laura told her. "He can draw a box, a ball and a happy face. Danny, draw something for Aunt Kathy."

So Daniel drew a picture. But everyone was very surprised when he didn't draw a box or a ball or a happy face — he drew a fairy instead!